Grayslake Area Public Library District
Grayslake, Illinois

1. A fine will be charged on each book which is not returned when it is due.

2. All injuries to books beyond reasonable wear and all losses shall be made good to the satisfaction of the Librarian.

3. Each borrower is held responsible for all books drawn on his card and for all fines accruing on the same.

DEMCO

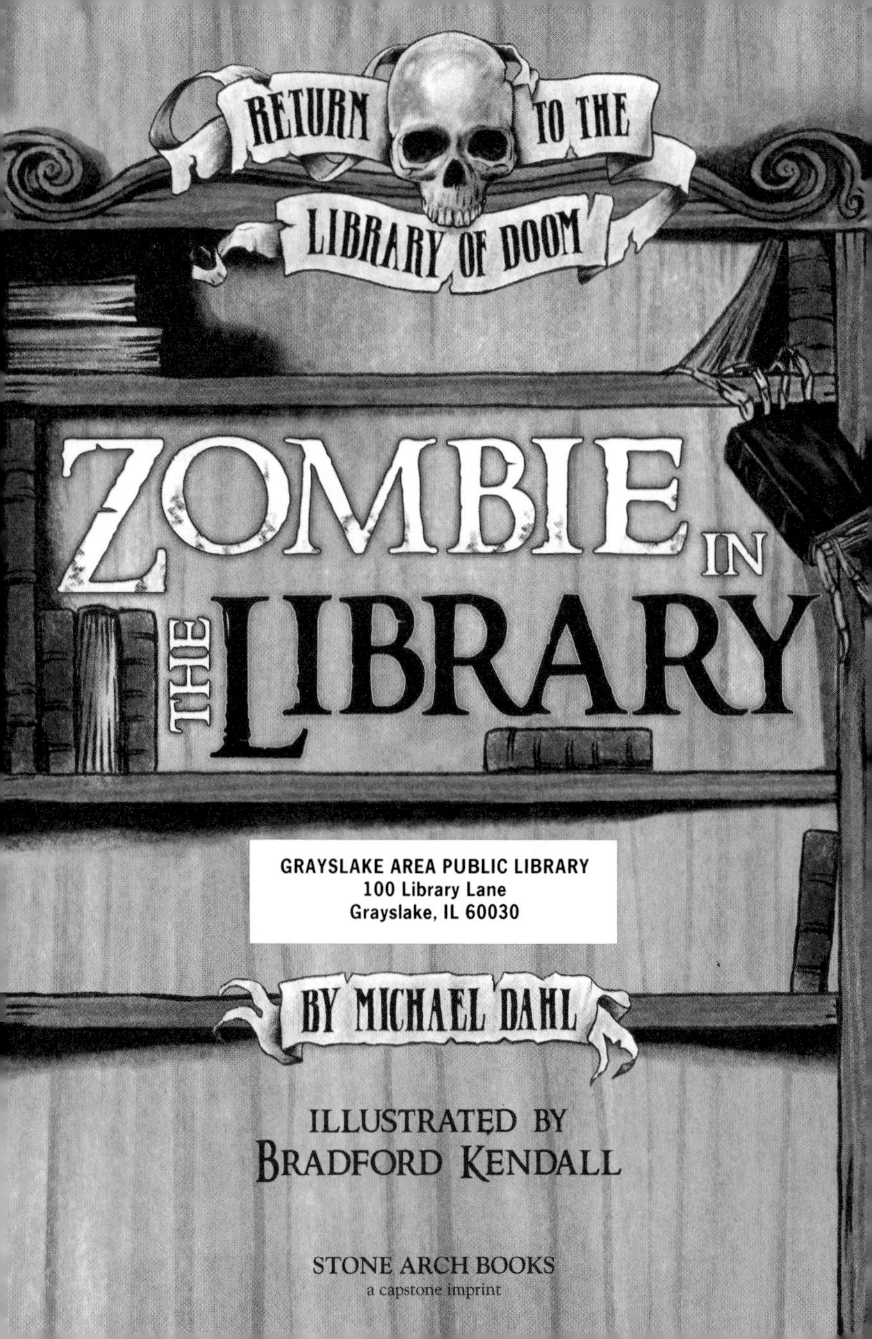

RETURN TO THE
LIBRARY OF DOOM

ZOMBIE IN THE LIBRARY

BY MICHAEL DAHL

ILLUSTRATED BY
BRADFORD KENDALL

STONE ARCH BOOKS
a capstone imprint

ZONE BOOKS ARE PUBLISHED BY
STONE ARCH BOOKS
A CAPSTONE IMPRINT
151 GOOD COUNSEL DRIVE, P.O. BOX 669
MANKATO, MINNESOTA 56002
WWW.CAPSTONEPUB.COM

LIBRARY OF CONGRESS CATALOGING-IN-PUBLICATION DATA
DAHL, MICHAEL.
  ZOMBIE IN THE LIBRARY / WRITTEN BY MICHAEL DAHL ;
ILLUSTRATED BY BRADFORD KENDALL.
       P. CM. -- (RETURN TO THE LIBRARY OF DOOM)
  ISBN 978-1-4342-2145-2 (LIBRARY BINDING)
 (1. ZOMBIES--FICTION. 2. LIBRARIES--FICTION. 3. HORROR
STORIES.) I. KENDALL, BRADFORD, ILL. II. TITLE.
  PZ7.D15134ZO 2011
  (FIC)--DC22   2010004107

ART DIRECTOR: KAY FRASER
GRAPHIC DESIGNER: HILARY WACHOLZ
PRODUCTION SPECIALIST: MICHELLE BIEDSCHEID

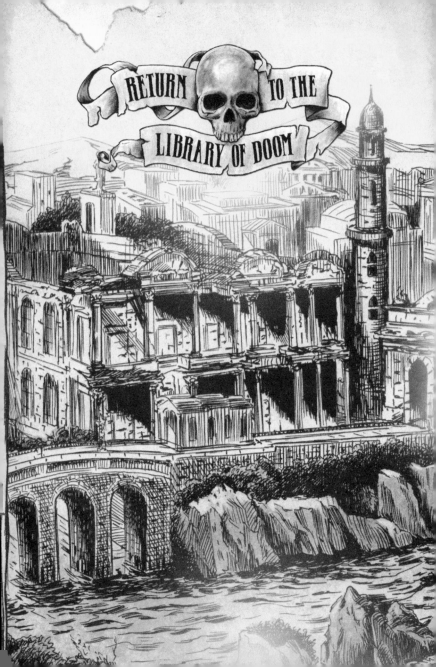

Behold the Library of Doom! The world's largest collection of deadly and dangerous books. Only the Librarian can prevent these books from falling into the hands of those who would use them for evil.

ARE BOOKS ALIVE OR DEAD? OR ARE THEY SOMETHING ELSE . . . ?

Chapter 1

LIGHTNING

Adam stands on his front
porch and stares at the **STORM**.

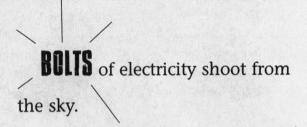

BOLTS of electricity shoot from the sky.

Lightning **DANCES** along the horizon.

"It's alive!" says a woman's voice.

Adam's mother steps out on the porch.

She stands beside her son.

"It looks alive, doesn't it?" she says, staring at the LIGHTNING.

Adam nods.

"Sorry, Adam," she says. "I guess we're not going into town tonight."

"But the **SALE** —" Adam says.

"I'm sure the **library** will move their sale to tomorrow night," says his mother. "That storm is just too fierce," she adds. "Besides, don't you already have enough books?"

?

?

?

Chapter 2

MONSTER BOOK

Adam puts his hands in his pockets.

In one of his pockets, he can feel the **DOLLAR** bills he's been saving.
$ $

He was planning to buy a special book for his mother's birthday.

Adam knows his mother likes books about old **MONSTER** movies. Books like that are too expensive.

But a few days ago Adam was at the library.

He saw the **PERFECT** book for his mother.

The book was filled with **old** photos.

It had chapters on vampires, phantoms, werewolves, and zombies.

It had a photo from his mom's favorite **SCARY** movie, *The Library of Doom.*

The hero was a monster hunter who wore dark glasses, even at night.

"Sorry, Adam," said a library worker.

"You can't **CHECK** out that book.
It's part of the sale we're having in a
few days."

Sale? thought Adam. That was even
better.

Now he could afford that **BOOK** for his mother's present.

"I'll put it aside," said the worker.

"You can buy it at the sale on Friday **NIGHT**."

It is Friday night.

The powerful **LIGHTNING** storm
is keeping everyone home.

Adam frowns.

He figures his mother is right.

No one will be at the town library tonight.

But Adam's mother is **WRONG**.

Chapter 3

THE UNWANTED

A shadow shuffles along the halls of the library.

The shadow is pushing a broom. It is Logan, the library's part-time janitor.

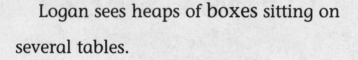

Logan sees heaps of boxes sitting on several tables.

He **STOPS**.

"More garbage!" he says to himself. "Why didn't someone tell me?"

The boxes are not garbage. The books for tonight's sale are inside the boxes.

They were never unpacked. The librarian had left early because of the STORM.

Logan carries the heavy boxes outside.

He **HURLS** them into a metal trash bin, one by one.

The book that Adam wants to buy falls from a box.

It lands on the bottom of the bin.

It is buried beneath hundreds of other
used books.

Logan *throws* the last box into the bin.

Then he pulls down the **HEAVY** metal lid. "What a pain!" he says.

The lightning storm rages overhead.

Logan heads toward the **library**.

CRACK!

A bolt of lightning **HITS** the
metal trash bin.

A loud grinding noise **echoes** through the alley.

"What was that?" he yells. "Who's there?"

He sees steam **RISING** from the trash bin. Something is moving inside the bin.

Slowly, the metal lid rises.

Logan **screams**.

A book, shaped like a claw, is lifting the lid.

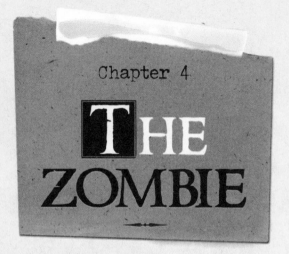

Chapter 4
THE ZOMBIE

Logan *runs* back inside the library.

From a window, he stares out at the trash bin.

A human-sized creature **CRAWLS** over the side of the bin.

The creature has no face. No eyes, no nose, no ears.

There is just a **HOLE** where its mouth should be.

The **CREATURE** reaches inside the bin and pulls out a book.

It holds it up to the hole in its face.

Logan thinks the creature is **EATING** the book.

The creature **pulls** out another book.

And another one.

It **CHEWS** at the books, and then tosses them aside.

Logan looks at the books that the creature has thrown away.

They are **SCATTERED** in the alley.

Lightning keeps flashing overhead.

Logan blinks his eyes. *I must be tired,* he thinks. *This can't be happening.*

Two of the books are **growing** legs.

SKINNY, papery legs sprout from the bottom of the book covers.

Thin arms are growing from the sides.

The living books **waddle** toward the library.

Suddenly, the human-sized creature points at Logan.

The pages of its face **FLIP** angrily back and forth.

The creature roars.

Chapter 5

BOOK ZOMBIES

Adam gets his bike out of the garage.

The lightning **won't stop** me from riding my bike, Adam thinks.

His bicycle's tires are **RUBBER**. *Rubber tires protect against electricity*, he tells himself. *Right?*

He is sure the **LIBRARY** will still have its sale.

The STORM won't stop people who live in town, Adam thinks.

And what if Mom's book is sold?

If I don't show up **tonight**, the librarian might sell it to someone else.

The library doors are **LOCKED** when he arrives.

There are lights on inside.

Adam **knocks**. No one answers.

Adam gets back on his bike. Maybe there is another door in the back.

As he turns into the alley, Adam runs into someone. "Sorry!" cries Adam.

Then he looks at the
STRANGER.

The stranger has NO eyes. There is a book where its face should be.

The pages of the face **flip** open,

one by one.

Adam sees pictures of monsters.
Vampires. Phantoms. Werewolves.
ZOMBIES.

The creature holds its arms out. It
lunges toward Adam.

Adam hears a **screech** behind
him.

A pickup truck has turned into the alley. Logan is **GRIPPING** the wheel.

"Get in!" he yells at Adam.

Adam throws himself at the truck's door. He **LEAPS** inside.

The faceless creature **CLAWS** at the window.

The walking books begin climbing into the truck's bed.

"Get off my truck!" yells Logan.

"We need to get <u>out of here</u>," whispers Adam.

Four more books **CLIMB** onto the

hood of the truck like fat spiders.

Chapter 6

LIGHTNING ROD

"I can't see where I'm going!"

Logan shouts.

The truck BOUNCES up and down.

"Oh no!" yells Adam. "That thing's in the truck!"

A **SHADOWY** figure stands in the bed behind them.

Lightning **FLASHES** in the alley.

It was stupid to come here, Adam thinks to himself. *I should have listened to Mom. I should have come tomorrow. No book is worth this!*

A man's face presses against the back .

The man wears **dark** sunglasses.

Adam recognizes him. It is the same man from his mother's favorite movie.

It is the LIBRARIAN.

"Some books are worth it," says the man. "Now, hold on!"

Suddenly, white-hot **LIGHTNING** fills the air. A bolt of electricity shoots through the truck.

"Whoa!" yells Logan. "What's happening?"

Adam looks out the back window.
The **BOOK ZOMBIE** is gone.

The bed of the truck is full of ashy
flakes, blowing in the wind.

Adam sees a <u>book</u> lying in the
middle of the ashes.

It is his mother's book.

The wind *BLOWS* the pages
open to a photo.

It shows the hero from the *Library
of Doom* flying through the SKY.

In a **BLAZE** of lightning, Adam
sees the man with the sunglasses.

He is flying over the library.

"Rubber tires," mutters Logan. "I think the rubber tires **SAVED** us from getting fried."

Adam knows it was **MORE** than the tires.

He feels the dollar bills still shoved into his pocket. He had saved up the money to buy his mother's present.

Tonight, his mother's present **SAVED** him.

AUTHOR

Michael Dahl is the author of more than 200 books for children and young adults. He has won the AEP Distinguished Achievement Award three times for his nonfiction. His Finnegan Zwake mystery series was shortlisted twice by the Anthony and Agatha awards. He has also written the Library of Doom series. He is a featured speaker at conferences around the country on graphic novels and high-interest books for boys.

ILLUSTRATOR

Bradford Kendall has enjoyed drawing for as long as he can remember. As a boy, he loved to read comic books and watch old monster movies. He graduated from Rhode Island School of Design with a BFA in Illustration. He has owned his own commercial art business since 1983, and lives in Providence, Rhode Island, with his wife, Leigh, and their two children Lily and Stephen. They also have a cat named Hansel and a dog named Gretel.

GLOSSARY

creature (KREE-chur)—a living being

electricity (i-lek-TRISS-uh-tee)—electrical power or an electrical current

fierce (FIHRSS)—violent or dangerous; very strong or extreme

horizon (huh-RYE-zuhn)—the line where the sky and the earth or sea seem to meet

lunges (LUHNJ-iz)—moves forward quickly and suddenly

protect (pruh-TEKT)—to guard or keep something safe from harm, attack, or injury

rages (RAYJ-iz)—is violent or noisy

recognizes (REK-uhg-nize-iz)—sees someone and knows who they are

rubber (RUHB-ur)—a substance made from the milky sap of a rubber tree or produced artificially. Rubber is strong, elastic, and waterproof, and is used for making tires, balls, boots, etc.

sprout (SPROUT)—start to grow

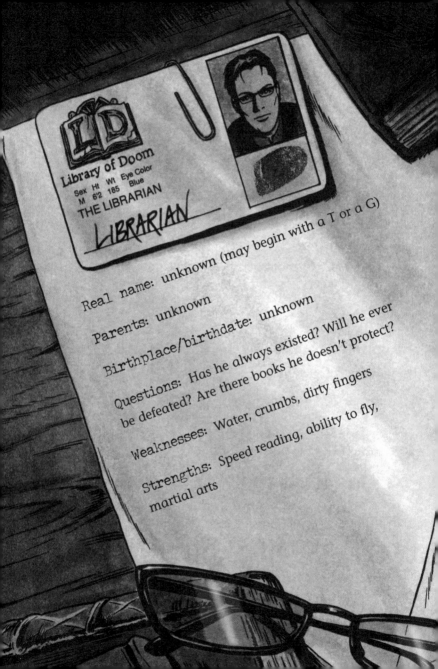

Library of Doom

Sex Ht Wt Eye Color
M 6'2 185 Blue

THE LIBRARIAN

LIBRARIAN

Real name: unknown (may begin with a T or a G)

Parents: unknown

Birthplace/birthdate: unknown

Questions: Has he always existed? Will he ever be defeated? Are there books he doesn't protect?

Weaknesses: Water, crumbs, dirty fingers

Strengths: Speed reading, ability to fly, martial arts

Library of Doom

Sex Ht Wt Eye Color
F 5'6 150 Brown

THE SPECIALIST

Specialist

Real name: Sophia (last name unknown)

Parents: unknown

Birthplace/birthdate: America, 20th century

Questions: What is her role in protecting the Librarian? Can she be stopped?

Weaknesses: Bad listeners

Strengths: Does not need sleep, can research anything

BOOK ZOMBIE

The Book Zombie that Logan and Adam encountered in the library was not the first Book Zombie to face the Librarian. In fact, dozens of Book Zombies have been spotted, usually in Tornado Alley—the area that spans the middle of the United States from South Dakota to Texas.

Usually seen during large electrical storms, Book Zombies are known for their speed and fearfulness. It is not known why they emerge during thunderstorms. However, the only thing known to destroy them is a large bolt of electricity, like from lightning. When the Librarian can make it in time, he can harness the lightning and destroy the Book Zombie. But there will always be more . . .

DISCUSSION QUESTIONS

1. Do you think Adam will get in trouble for going to the library in the STORM? Why or why not?

2. What did you think about the title of this book? Does it match what you felt when you read the story? Can you think of other titles that would be a GOOD fit for this book?

3. Who is the Librarian? What is the Library of Doom?

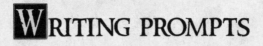RITING PROMPTS

1. In this book, Adam is in a dangerous situation. Write about a time when you experienced **DANGER**.

2. Pretend you're Adam. Write a letter to a friend, explaining what happened at the **library**.

3. **CREATE** a cover for a book. It can be this book or another book you like, or a made-up book. Don't forget to write the information on the back, and include the author and illustrator names!